Elizabeth
the Jubilee
Fairy

ORCHARD BOOKS
338 Euston Road, London NW1 3BH
Orchard Books Australia
Level 17/207 Kent Street, Sydney, NSW 2000
A Paperback Original

First published in 2012 by Orchard Books

© 2012 Rainbow Magic Limited.
A HIT Entertainment company. Rainbow Magic
is a trademark of Rainbow Magic Limited.
Reg. U.S. Pat. & Tm. Off. And other countries.

HiT entertainment

Illustrations © Orchard Books 2012

A CIP catalogue record for this book is available
from the British Library.

ISBN 978 1 40832 384 7

1 3 5 7 9 10 8 6 4 2

Printed in Great Britain

Orchard Books is a division of Hachette Children's Books,
an Hachette UK company

www.hachette.co.uk

Elizabeth
the Jubilee
Fairy

by Daisy Meadows

ORCHARD

www.rainbowmagic.co.uk

The Fairyland Palace

The Icicle

River Bank

Royal Boat

Tower of London

Jack Frost's Ice Castle

Goblin Town

River Thames

It's a time for celebration
All across the goblin nation
Because I've been king for years, you see
So now this is my jubilee!

Who will organise my special day?
My goblins are useless, but I'll find a way!
Elizabeth's magic will guarantee
That I have a fabulous jubilee!

Contents

The Sovereign's Sceptre

"The Sovereign's Sceptre," Kirsty read out, staring wide-eyed at the glass case in front of her. Inside was a long golden sceptre with a diamond cross on top. Below the cross was an enormous, pear-shaped diamond that glowed in the lights. "Rachel, isn't that *amazing*?"

9

"Amazing!" Rachel agreed. She was completely dazzled by all the Crown Jewels on display – the crowns, the sceptres, the orbs and the rings.

The girls were visiting the Tower of London with their parents, and they'd enjoyed seeing the Yeoman Warders in their colourful costumes and the big black ravens who lived inside the walls of the Tower. Then they had queued to see the Crown Jewels, along with hundreds of other tourists. Later, they were going to join the crowds gathering on the banks of the River Thames to watch the start of the queen's Diamond Jubilee celebrations. The girls could hardly wait!

"What does the guidebook say, Dad?" Rachel asked.

Mr Walker consulted
his book. "The sceptre
was made for King
Charles the Second,
and our present
queen carried
it when she
was crowned at
Westminster Abbey
sixty years ago," he replied.

"It looks heavy!" Rachel said.

"And is that a *real* diamond?" Kirsty
asked, staring at the huge, glittering stone
in awe.

"Yes, it's called the Great Star of
Africa," Mr Walker explained. "It's one
of nine diamonds cut from the Cullinan
Diamond, which is the largest that's ever
been found."

"Goodness me!" said Mrs Tate. "It must be worth a lot of money."

Rachel glanced at her watch. "We won't be late for the start of the Jubilee Pageant, will we, Mum?" she asked a little anxiously.

"No, we've got plenty of time," Mrs Walker replied.

"The Jubilee Pageant sounds quite spectacular," Mr Walker remarked. "There'll be hundreds of different boats sailing down the River Thames, all decorated with streamers and flags."

"Apparently there'll be musicians playing on some of the boats, too," Mrs

Tate said. "And there are also barges carrying fireworks that'll be set off as they sail along."

"Great!" Kirsty exclaimed happily. "Wouldn't it be *brilliant* to be a passenger on one of the boats, Rachel?"

Rachel nodded.

"There *are* some special boats for members of the public," Mrs Walker told them. "The people will all be waving flags. It really will be a wonderful sight."

Mr Tate was still studying the Sovereign's Sceptre. "Didn't someone try to steal the Crown Jewels once?" he asked.

Rachel's dad flipped through his guidebook. "Ah, here we are!" he said. "Yes, it happened in 1671..."

Kirsty was very interested in what Rachel's dad was saying, but suddenly her attention was caught by something else. She could see a strange, glowing light coming from a narrow window nearby. Kirsty frowned. It was a warm day but the sky was overcast and the sun wasn't shining. So what *was* that bright little light?

Kirsty nudged Rachel. "Look!" she murmured, looking over at the glow.

"Oh!" Rachel let out a tiny gasp of delight. "Kirsty, could it be—?"

Quickly the girls slipped away and went over to the window.

Now they could see a tiny figure in the
centre of the light, waving at them.

"A fairy!" Kirsty whispered, thrilled.

The fairy beckoned them to come
closer. She had short,
brown, glossy hair
with a shiny orb-
shaped clip. Her
Union Jack-
patterned dress
sparkled with
hundreds of tiny
diamonds and
she had rather

lovely, diamond-shaped wings. Her tiny
shoes were bright blue with dazzling
golden hearts on the toes.

"Girls, we haven't met properly before,"
the fairy said in a sweet voice. "I'm

Elizabeth the Jubilee Fairy!"

"The *Jubilee* Fairy?" Rachel and Kirsty repeated, surprised.

Elizabeth nodded. "I know that today is a very special day for your queen," she said, her eyes twinkling. "But it's also a *very* special day in Fairyland. You see, it's exactly one thousand, one hundred years since King Oberon and Queen Titania were crowned!"

"That's fantastic!" Kirsty exclaimed.

"Are you having jubilee celebrations, too?" Rachel asked.

16

"Oh, yes!" Elizabeth replied. "For
the last week the king and queen have
been on a grand tour around their
fairy kingdom. We've all decorated our
houses, and Bertram the frog footman is
in charge of a souvenir book. It's being
passed around so that
all the fairies can
write messages
for the king
and queen."

"What a
good idea!"
said Kirsty.

"The Party
Fairies have
organised jubilee lunches,
too," Elizabeth went on. "They've set
up tables outside, just like your street

17

parties! And today is the day of the
River Pageant, which *should* be the most
special celebration of all…" Elizabeth
sighed deeply.

"What's the matter?" Kirsty asked,
concerned.

"Jack Frost has done something
terrible!" Elizabeth explained sadly.
"Something that will ruin all our
celebrations in Fairyland, *and* yours here
in the human world."

Kirsty and Rachel looked horrified.

"That's why I'm here." Elizabeth
looked pleadingly at the girls. "Will you
come to Fairyland and help me put
things right? I'll explain everything as
soon as we get there."

"Of course we will!" Rachel cried, as
Kirsty nodded eagerly.

Looking relieved, Elizabeth lifted her
wand. "Thank you. There's not a moment
to lose!" And, with a flick of Elizabeth's
wrist, a cloud of fairy dust surrounded
Rachel and Kirsty. In an instant the
girls were fairy-size, and then Elizabeth's
magic whirled them away to Fairyland.

Fairyland River Pageant

A moment later Kirsty and Rachel found themselves with Elizabeth and crowds of other fairies on the bank of a wide, blue river. All the fairies were chattering excitedly to each other. The girls could see boats moored all along the bank, bobbing gently up and down on the crystal-clear water.

"Look, all the boats are beautifully decorated," Rachel said to Kirsty. "They look like floats at a carnival."

"See that one with the pink sails?" Kirsty pointed out. "It's really glittering in the sunshine."

Rachel looked more closely. "That's because the whole boat is covered with precious stones!" she exclaimed. "Look, the Jewel Fairies are on board! I can see India the Moonstone Fairy and Lucy the Diamond Fairy."

"Every fairy group has decorated its own boat for the River Pageant," Elizabeth told them as Kirsty spotted the Fun Day Fairies' boat, their magical flags hanging from the masts. "Today is the actual day of the king and queen's jubilee, so the River Pageant is the biggest celebration of all."

"What's going to happen?" asked Kirsty.

"See the Royal Boat?" Elizabeth pointed her wand at a beautiful boat of polished wood with golden sails.

"King Oberon and Queen Titania will board it very soon, and then sail to the mouth of the river, with all of the other boats following behind. The Ocean Fairies and their sea creatures will perform a show in the water and then, when evening falls, there'll be beacons lit all along the coast, and a grand fireworks display out at sea."

"It sounds wonderful," said Rachel.

"It *will* be wonderful – if we can stop Jack Frost from spoiling everything!" Elizabeth replied.

"Tell us what happened," said Kirsty.

Elizabeth drew the girls aside a little. "Well," she began in a low voice, "Jack Frost was invited to join the celebrations and take part in the River Pageant. There's his boat."

Elizabeth pointed to a boat made of ice moored a short distance away from the others. The boat was called *The Icicle*, and it had ice-blue sails with enormous pictures of Jack Frost's face on them. The girls could see the goblin crew on board, running around on the slippery, frozen deck.

"Was Jack Frost pleased?" Rachel wanted to know.

Elizabeth shook her head. "Not at all!" she said. "He grudgingly agreed to take part, but ever since, he's got grumpier every day. This morning I was helping the fairies to decorate their boats when Jack Frost arrived and threw a *real* tantrum!"

"Why?" Kirsty asked.

"Because Jack Frost thinks *he* should have a celebration, too!" Elizabeth sighed. "He yelled that he didn't know

exactly how many years he's been ruling
over the goblins, but it's high time that
he got presents and cake and lots of
attention! Then he stormed off."

Rachel looked
worried. "So
do you think
Jack Frost
is planning
to disrupt
the River
Pageant?"

"He already
has," Elizabeth replied sadly. "Because
before Jack Frost left, he stole my
Diamond Sceptre! And without the
magic of my sceptre, all jubilee events in
both the human and the fairy worlds will
be completely ruined!"

Rachel and Kirsty looked at Elizabeth in dismay.

"I'd put my sceptre down on the river bank for a moment while I helped Grace the Glitter Fairy pin up a streamer on the Party Fairies' boat," Elizabeth continued. "Then, when I turned back, it was gone! Jack Frost probably thinks that if he has the sceptre, then the goblins will organise some wonderful celebrations for *him*!"

"It would be terrible if King Oberon, Queen Titania and our queen couldn't celebrate their jubilees properly because of Jack Frost's selfishness!" Rachel said.

Elizabeth glanced at the crowds of excited fairies. "No one knows what's happened except me," she whispered. "Everyone would be *very* worried, and I don't want to spoil the party atmosphere."

"Then there's only one thing we can do," Rachel declared. "We have to get the Diamond Sceptre back!"

"And *before* anyone realises it's missing!" Kirsty agreed.

No Fairies Allowed!

"I knew I could count on you, girls!" Elizabeth said gratefully. "Where shall we start?"

Before Rachel or Kirsty could reply, there was a shout from one of the fairies on the river bank.

"Look! The river water is draining away!" she cried.

Elizabeth and the girls gazed at the river. They could see that the level of the water was going down rapidly – just as if someone had pulled out a plug in the river bed!

All the fairies looked very worried.

"The water's far too shallow now," called Megan the Monday Fairy from the Fun Day Fairies' boat. "We'll get stuck in the mud on the river bed if we try to set sail."

"Maybe the water level will rise again before the king and queen arrive," Fern the Green Fairy said hopefully. She was standing on the Rainbow Fairies' boat with its multi-coloured sails.

"How will we know when it's our turn to set sail?" asked Emily the Emerald Fairy anxiously. "Has someone got a list with the sailing order?"

"Bertram has it," Pearl the Cloud Fairy replied.

"No, he doesn't," Saskia the Salsa Fairy chimed in. "He said one of the Party Fairies has it."

"*We* don't have it!" chorused the Party Fairies from their boat, which was hung with glittery paper chains and balloons.

Kirsty and Rachel glanced at each other in dismay. Everything was going horribly wrong already! The sky was clouding over and the sun had disappeared. On the Weather Fairies' boat, Goldie the Sunshine Fairy was looking very upset.

"Why isn't my magic working properly?" she asked miserably.

Suddenly Milly the River Fairy appeared on the deck of the Royal Boat, looking desperately worried.

"There's a leak in the boat!" the fairy gasped. "Quick, we *must* bail the water out before King Oberon and Queen Titania arrive!"

34

Swiftly, a group of fairies formed a
chain on the river bank and began
passing buckets to and fro.

"This is all happening because my
Diamond Sceptre is missing," Elizabeth
whispered to the girls. "We *must* get it
back from Jack Frost."

"I wonder if he's on his boat?" asked
Kirsty. She looked over at *The Icicle*, but
all she could see was goblins.

"It's a good place to start!" Rachel replied. "Even if Jack Frost isn't there, we *might* find clues to where he's gone."

Quickly, Elizabeth, Kirsty and Rachel flew along the river bank. They could see the goblin crew still sliding around on *The Icicle*'s deck, but they didn't appear to be getting very much done. They were arguing about everything from how to tie a knot in the ropes to who should count the life jackets.

Then, as Elizabeth and the girls got closer, one of the goblins spotted them. Scowling, he grabbed a megaphone.

"NO FAIRIES ALLOWED!" the goblin yelled through the megaphone. "NO FAIRIES ALLOWED ON THIS BOAT!"

Elizabeth and the girls stopped in midair, fluttering their wings.

"What now?" Kirsty asked anxiously.

"Maybe the goblins will let us onto the boat if they think we're something to do with the River Pageant," Rachel suggested.

"Brilliant idea!" Elizabeth agreed. Lifting her wand, she surrounded herself and the girls with dazzling sparkles of fairy magic. Now all three of them were wearing glittering gold badges, and each badge had *Official Jubilee Inspector* written on it.

"Let's go!" said Elizabeth, and once more they flew towards *The Icicle*.

"NO FAIRIES ALLOWED!" the

goblin with the megaphone roared again. "NO—" He stopped short when Elizabeth pointed to her badge.

"We're here to inspect your boat," Elizabeth said.

"We're checking that all the boats in the River Pageant are looking their best," Rachel added.

The rest of the goblin crew rushed over to see what was going on.

"These fairies say they've got to

inspect our boat," the goblin with the megaphone told them.

"You won't be able to take part in the pageant otherwise," Kirsty said. She tried not to look too eager. Would the goblins let them on board or not?

On Board 'The Icicle'

"Come on, then!" said the biggest of the goblin crew, and Kirsty breathed a sigh of relief. "You'll soon see that ours is the most beautiful boat in the whole River Pageant!"

"IT'S EVEN MORE BEAUTIFUL THAN THAT SILLY ROYAL THING!" boomed the goblin with the megaphone, as the others slid around the icy deck, roaring with laughter.

The big goblin strutted off across the deck with Elizabeth and the girls, and the other goblins followed. It was freezing cold on the boat, and long glittering icicles hung from the masts.

"See our tall sails?" the big goblin boasted, pointing upwards.

"We'll be faster than any of the other boats in the pageant!"

"Yes, very nice," Rachel agreed, trying not to shiver.

42

As the big goblin led them all over the
deck, she, Kirsty and Elizabeth kept
glancing around, trying to spot any clues
about where Jack Frost and the Diamond
Sceptre might be. But they couldn't see
anything.

"Can we go below deck?" Kirsty asked.

The big goblin took them through a
narrow hatch and down some icy steps
into the bottom
of the boat.
The other
goblins
came too,
pushing
and shoving
their way
through the
hatch.

"This is Jack Frost's cabin," the big goblin announced proudly, flinging open the nearest door.

Elizabeth and the girls flew into the cabin. There was an ornate bed carved from a block of ice, as well as a desk and a captain's chair. Immediately, Kirsty noticed that there was a leaflet lying open on the chair seat. She wondered how she could get a look at it without making the goblins suspicious.

All the goblins were now trying to get inside the cabin at once, and the big goblin was getting annoyed.

"Go up on deck!" he ordered them.

"SHAN'T!" roared the goblin with the megaphone. The big goblin was furious and he began shoving the others out of the cabin door. Meanwhile, Kirsty

44

seized her chance and fluttered over to
the chair.

"Oh, it's a programme of the Fairyland
jubilee events," Kirsty murmured as she
stared down at the leaflet. Rachel and
Elizabeth zoomed over to join her. "And
look, Jack Frost has written something
on it."

The programme page listed all the wonderful events that were taking place in Fairyland during the week. Jack Frost had circled a jubilee lunch with an ice-blue pen. Then next to the circle he'd scrawled, in spiky writing, *I want one of these!*

"So Jack Frost wants his own street party!" Elizabeth exclaimed.

"But where?" Kirsty wondered.

"In the goblin town, I should think!" said Rachel.

"Of course!" Elizabeth agreed. "We'll go there right away!" And, with a wave of her wand, a burst of fairy magic made them small and whisked them out of an open porthole and across Fairyland to Jack Frost's Ice Kingdom.

A few seconds later the three friends

arrived in the goblin town. The town
was at the bottom of the hill where Jack
Frost's Ice Castle stood, and it was a grey,
miserable-looking place
with narrow little
houses and a
freezing chill
in the air.
There were
lots of goblins
scurrying here
and there,
and Elizabeth,
Kirsty and
Rachel quickly
flew out of sight
behind a frozen, leafless tree.

"It looks like the whole town is in
uproar!" Kirsty whispered.

47

At that moment a group of goblins ran past, stumbling and tripping over each other's big feet, as well as their own.

"Quick!" one of them gasped. "Jack Frost wants his jubilee celebration lunch NOW!"

"What are we celebrating?" panted a second goblin.

"That Jack Frost is the best boss EVER!" the first goblin replied. "And we'll be in big trouble if we don't make a HUGE effort!"

"Oh, no," groaned the other goblin. "Here he comes now!"

Kirsty, Rachel and Elizabeth peeped out from behind the tree. They saw Jack Frost marching down the street, shouting orders at the goblins around him. In his hand was a long golden sceptre with a

glittering diamond on
top of it.

"It's my sceptre!"
Elizabeth whispered.

"You!" Jack Frost
pointed the sceptre
at a gang of goblins.
"Have you lit the
beacons to celebrate my jubilee?"

"Yes, sir," the goblins chorused.

"Then start bringing tables and chairs
to the town square for my jubilee lunch!"
Jack Frost snapped. Then he strode off,
swinging the sceptre.

"We have to get my sceptre back or the
jubilee events everywhere will be ruined!"
Elizabeth told the girls.

"But how can we get the sceptre away
from Jack Frost?" asked Rachel.

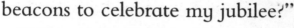

49

Goblin Officials

"Maybe Rachel and I could do what we did before, but pretend to be goblin officials this time?" Kirsty suggested. "Then we might be able to get Jack Frost to hand over the sceptre."

"Great idea, Kirsty," Rachel agreed. "Elizabeth, could you magic up some goblin disguises for us?"

Elizabeth smiled and pointed her wand at them. Instantly a mist of fairy dust turned Rachel and Kirsty bright green from head to toe. The girls couldn't help laughing, even though it wasn't the first time they'd pretended to be goblins. They were now wearing caps, long coats and shoes that were much too big. Each of them had an ice-blue badge with *Official Jubilee Inspector* on it, pinned to their coats.

"The coats will hide your wings, and the hats will cover your eyes, so no one will be able to tell that you aren't real goblins," Elizabeth explained.

Jack Frost was now in the town square shouting instructions at the goblins who were arranging tables for the party. Quickly, Rachel and Kirsty hurried over to him. Elizabeth followed them, keeping out of sight behind the frozen trees.

"Mr Frost!" Rachel called. "May we have a word with you?"

Jack Frost glared at the girls. "What do you want?" he demanded, peering at their badges. "You should be busy organising my jubilee celebration, not being a nuisance!"

"We work for the goblin town mayor, Mr Frost," Kirsty said quickly, glancing at the Diamond Sceptre in Jack Frost's hand. It glittered magically in the pale, wintry light.

"We'd like to put the Jubilee Fairy's

sceptre on display here in the town square to commemorate this *very* special day," Rachel explained.

"The day our wonderful ruler, Jack Frost, got the better of those pesky fairies once and for all!" Kirsty added.

"What a wonderful idea!" Jack Frost exclaimed, looking thrilled.

"Here, take it."

Kirsty felt her heart pounding with excitement as Jack Frost held out the sceptre to her. But then there was a shout from one of the goblins in the street.

"Fairy!" he yelled, pointing at the tree where Elizabeth was hiding.

Desperately Rachel lunged forward and tried to grab the sceptre, but Jack Frost dodged her and stepped aside. As a group of goblins captured Elizabeth and held her prisoner, Jack Frost eyed the girls suspiciously.

"You were trying to trick me!" he roared.

"Run, Rachel!" Kirsty gasped. If they could get away, at least then they might be able to help Elizabeth, Kirsty thought.

The girls made a run for it, but Jack Frost pointed his wand at them, firing ice bolt after ice bolt in their direction. His magic knocked the girls off their feet, stripping away the coats, caps and shoes they were wearing, and making their green skin fade.

"More fairies!" Jack Frost snapped.

"I knew it!" He stared coldly at Elizabeth, Kirsty and Rachel. "Now, how shall I make you pay for gate-crashing my jubilee celebrations?"

Suddenly, a loud, ear-splitting noise echoed down the street. The next moment a huge crowd of goblins marched towards them, singing out of tune at the tops of their voices:

Who's handsome, charming,
clever and grand?
Who's the best boss in the land?
It's Jack Frost, king of ice and snow,
Go, Jack, go, Jack, GO, GO, GO!

"STOP!" Jack Frost shouted, covering his ears. "That's terrible!"

The goblins looked very disappointed. One of the goblins was carrying a cake, and he stepped forward proudly, putting it down on the table in front of Jack Frost. Rachel and Kirsty could see that the cake had sunk in the middle and was burnt around the edges. Some of the other goblins were carrying plates of biscuits and jugs of water, and they put these down on the table, too.

"Is that it?" Jack Frost yelled, staring at

the food in disgust. "*This* is my special jubilee lunch?" He glared at Elizabeth. "Doesn't this stupid sceptre work?" he demanded sulkily.

"Of course it does," Elizabeth replied calmly. "But the magic of my sceptre only helps events to run smoothly. The organisation of the celebrations is done by everyone in the kingdom who wants to show their king and queen how much they love and respect them. It's the enthusiasm and imagination of these loyal subjects that make the celebrations so special."

Jack Frost frowned.

"And the fairies have been planning their jubilee events for months," Elizabeth went on. "You've only given your goblins a few hours."

"But you can still have a wonderful jubilee," Rachel said quickly. "*If* you give the sceptre back to Elizabeth."

"Elizabeth's magic can help you celebrate properly," Kirsty added. "And it'll mean that the River Pageant will be a success, too." She and Rachel both held their breath as Jack Frost looked thoughtful.

What would he say?

Three Jubilee Celebrations

"Very well!" Jack Frost said at last, and he handed the Diamond Sceptre to Elizabeth. The girls sighed with relief.

As soon as Elizabeth touched the sceptre, it shrank down to its proper size. Then Elizabeth waved her wand, chanting a spell:

63

It's a celebration day
A special time in every way,
So come and join our street party fun,
There's plenty of room for
EVERYONE!

Rachel and Kirsty could hardly believe their eyes when in an instant the whole town was completely transformed. The tables were now decorated with swags of blue and white silk, and they were piled high with sandwiches, sausage rolls, iced buns and cupcakes, together with frothy hot chocolate, marshmallows and jugs of lemonade. The goblins were all wearing paper crowns and carrying ice-blue flags with Jack Frost's face on them. Banners printed with Jack Frost's picture hung from the highest windows in the town square.

At one end of the square a large stage
had appeared, and Frosty's Gobolicious
Band were tuning their instruments,
preparing to perform. Rachel and Kirsty
grinned at each other as, chattering
excitedly, the goblins seated themselves
at the tables.

"There are presents for everyone," Elizabeth announced, pointing her wand at heaps of beautifully wrapped parcels near the stage. Then, as Frosty's Gobolicious Band began to play, fireworks all around the square shot sparkling fountains of snow up into the air.

"I think Jack Frost's enjoying himself!" Rachel whispered to Kirsty.

Jack Frost was beaming from ear to
ear. He jumped up onto the stage to join
the band and
announced,
"I'm going
to sing my
new song,
'Jubilee
Rap'!"
The
goblins
cheered.

"Girls,
we must go," Elizabeth said when Jack
Frost had finished his song. "It's time
for the River Pageant to begin back in
Fairyland."

"Wait for me!" Jack Frost called. He
jumped onto an ice bolt and followed

Elizabeth and the girls as
they whizzed off back
to Fairyland.

When they arrived,
Rachel and Kirsty
saw that King
Oberon and Queen
Titania were already
climbing aboard the
Royal Boat. The fairies
cheered and waved colourful flags as the
king and queen took their seats.

"We're just in time!" Elizabeth said,
relieved. One wave of her wand, and
the river level rose up again. The sun
came out from behind the cloud, bathing
everything in a golden glow. Quickly,
Jack Frost joined his goblins on board
The Icicle.

68

"We've been invited to sail with the king and queen on the Royal Boat," Elizabeth told Rachel and Kirsty, who glanced at each other, thrilled. The three of them flew over to the boat and landed on the deck.

"Girls, how wonderful to see you!" Queen Titania exclaimed.

"We were hoping Elizabeth would invite you," said King Oberon with a smile.

"Congratulations on your jubilee!" the girls chorused excitedly as the Royal Boat moved off.

69

The fairies on the bank cheered and applauded as it sailed slowly down the river, the other boats, including *The Icicle*, in its wake. Rachel and Kirsty enjoyed waving at the crowds as they moved along. Then, as they drew near to the mouth of the river, Shannon and the other Ocean Fairies appeared, swimming towards the Royal Boat in sequence like synchronised swimmers. They were accompanied by dolphins, sea turtles, whales and other sea creatures, dipping and diving beneath the

waves and then surfacing again. Rachel
and Kirsty thought it was one of the
most wonderful sights they'd ever seen.

"It's time for you to go back to the
human world," Elizabeth told the girls
as night began to fall. The boats had
now made their way back to the river
bank, the beacons along the coast had
been lit and all the fairies were watching
spectacular fireworks explode into
rainbow-coloured sparks over the sea.
"You mustn't miss a moment of your
own jubilee celebrations! Thank you *so*
much for all your help."

"Goodbye, Elizabeth!" Rachel and
Kirsty called as a shower of sparkles
whisked them off their feet and
straight back to the Tower of London.
Time had stopped while they were in

Fairyland, so their parents were still looking at the spectacular Sovereign's Sceptre.

"Girls, it's time to make our way to watch the Jubilee Pageant," said Mrs Walker. "And we have something very exciting to tell you!"

"What is it?" Rachel asked eagerly.

"We're going to be on one of the passenger boats that's part of the Jubilee Pageant!" Mr Tate announced with a grin.

"We've been dying to tell you, but we wanted it to be a special surprise," Mrs Tate added as Mr Walker handed the girls a Union Jack flag each.

"Fantastic!" Kirsty gasped, her eyes shining. "I think the Diamond Jubilee celebrations are going to be *really* magical!"

As the girls followed their parents out of the Jewel Room, they glanced at each other in delight.

"Aren't we lucky, Rachel?" Kirsty whispered. "*Three* jubilee celebrations in one day!"

"Very lucky!" Rachel agreed, and the two girls shared a secret smile.

Now **Kirsty and Rachel**
must help...

Miley the Stylist Fairy

Read on for a sneak peek...

"What's that noise?" Rachel murmured
sleepily. She could hear a steady
pitter-patter sound on the roof of the tent
above her. Yawning, Rachel sat up in her
sleeping bag. At the same moment, her
best friend Kirsty stirred and opened her
eyes.

"Oh, it's *raining!*" Rachel exclaimed,
suddenly realising what the noise was.

Kirsty sat up, too. "Is that thunder?"
she asked a little nervously as a loud
rumbling echoed through the tent.

Rachel laughed. "No, that's my dad

snoring in the other bedroom!" she explained. Scrambling out of her sleeping bag, she went over to the tent's main entrance. Kirsty followed, and together the two girls peered out.

The site of the Rainspell Island Music Festival was awash with heavy rain. The sky was dark and threatening, and the grassy fields where the tents, stages and pop stars' trailers had been set up were already turning to mud.

"What a shame!" Kirsty remarked, "Especially when we had such brilliant weather yesterday."

"It doesn't matter whether it's sunny or rainy, though, does it?" Rachel reminded her. "We've still *got* to keep looking for the Pop Star Fairies' magical clefs!"

Kirsty nodded. "I wonder which

fairy we'll be helping today?" she said.

When the girls had arrived on Rainspell the day before, they'd discovered that Jack Frost and his goblins had stolen the Pop Star Fairies' clefs, the magical items that helped them look after pop music.

It was Jack Frost's ambition to be the richest and most famous pop star in the whole world, and he planned to use the power of the clefs to perform at the Rainspell Festival. Rachel and Kirsty had promised to help the fairies get the clefs back because without them, pop music in both the human and the fairy worlds would be spoilt for everyone. So far the girls, along with Jessie the Lyrics Fairy, Adele the Singing Coach Fairy and Vanessa the Dance Steps Fairy, had managed to rescue three of the clefs from the goblins who were hiding them.

"We saw three fantastic concerts yesterday, didn't we?" Rachel remarked as she and Kirsty went back to their sleeping area. "It was lucky Jessie, Adele and Vanessa got their clefs back in time, and that they each had *just* enough magic for The Angels, A-OK and Sasha Sharp to perform."

"But the Pop Star Fairies need *all* the clefs for things to be right again," Kirsty sighed. "And although we've seen the

Read Miley the Stylist Fairy to find out what adventures are in store for Kirsty and Rachel!

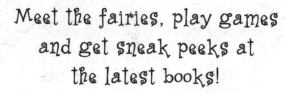

Meet the fairies, play games
and get sneak peeks at
the latest books!

www.rainbowmagicbooks.co.uk

There's fairy fun for everyone on
our wonderful website.
You'll find great activities, competitions, stories and
fairy profiles, and also a special newsletter.

Get 30% off all Rainbow Magic books at

www.rainbowmagicbooks.co.uk

Enter the code RAINBOW at the checkout.
Offer ends 31 December 2012.

Offer valid in United Kingdom and Republic of Ireland only.

Competition!

Elizabeth the Jubilee Fairy has created this special word wand just for you! Read the clues and write the answers in the boxes. The last letter of each word is the start of the next one. When you have all three answers, go online to enter.

1. Which human king was the sceptre made for?

2. What does Jack Frost steal from Elizabeth?

3. Which petal fairy looks after roses?

We will put all of the correct entries into a draw and select one winner to receive a special goody bag. You'll also star in a new Rainbow Magic story!

Enter online now at www.rainbowmagicbooks.co.uk

Meet the
Pop Star Fairies

Out Now!

Jessie
the Lyrics
Fairy

Adele
the Singing Coach
Fairy

Vanessa
the Dance Steps
Fairy

Out in June

Miley
the Stylist
Fairy

Frankie
the Make-up
Fairy

Rochelle
the Star Spotter
Fairy

Una
the Concert
Fairy

Kirsty and Rachel have to save Rainspell Island Music
Festival after Jack Frost steals the Pop Star Fairies'
musical clef necklaces!

www.rainbowmagicbooks.co.uk